HIS SEDUCTIVE SMILE

Jossette Devereaux

Full Moon Publishing, LLC
Glade Spring, VA
Fullmoonpublishingllc.com

ISBN: 1946232475
ISBN-13: 978-1946232472

I wake with that sweet sticky covering my body, my hair a matted mess, and a guy I barely know lying beside me sleeping heavily. My mouth waters as I notice the covers are pulled down to just above the top of his ass—too bad. It would be so nice to see more of that hot body in the light of the sun—the same gleaming sun that is illuminating his muscular lean back and arms. It is the body of an Adonis—so tan, so lean, hair a little below the collar being tussled, messy and light brown, and having the bluest of eyes that are currently covered with beautiful eyelids adorned with long black lashes.

The night is a blur—well except for the hours of hot sex with this gorgeous guy lying next to me—I'm not even certain where I am. Sitting up I rub my eyes, I stretch my arms and I slowly and quietly slip from under the sheets and make my way around the unfamiliar apartment until the bathroom emerges.

A claw foot bathtub— "Wow," is the only thing that goes through my mind. I admire its unique beauty. The porcelain on the inside of the tub is snow white

1

and flawless. The coal black exterior of the tub is painted to match the bathroom floor, which stands out against the stark white walls. Resting on intricately cast silver claw feet look amazing against the slick black marble floor tiles. The ivory towels are monogrammed with an ebony BMB. *What his full name is? I only know him as Bret.*

Turning the cool silver and porcelain handles of the faucet; I first turn on the hot water and let it run so that it can heat up. As room steams and I notice a message on the mirror—it simply says "You're amazing, Mia." *When did he do this? It is really sweet but at the same time kind of creepy.* I smile and shrug my shoulders. I think back to last night—amazing is the only word to describe it. It's so hard to believe I only met this man last night. If feels like I have known him forever. And it is so bizarre the way he did everything perfect—he did exactly what I like and did nothing that I dislike. It was like he had known me forever. This connection is so strange.

Sitting on the edge of the bathtub, the cool porcelain against my skin causes chill bumps. I ponder the connection that this man I just met and myself have. Reaching over slowly I turn the cold water handle on the faucet until the water reaches the perfect temperature—which is pretty hot. I don't like cold baths or showers; they have to be hot, very hot—so hot that my skin turns red.

When the water is perfect I slowly slip first one foot and then the other into the tub. The coolness of the bottom of the tub causes prickly chill bumps to cover my body. Porcelain warms up very slowly. I lay back and let the water continue to fill the tub. The faucet isn't that cold so I rest my feet on it. When the water fills almost to the top of the tub I raise up and turn both handles off—the room is quiet except for an occasional drip from the faucet. Lying back I close my eyes and let myself slip away and slide deep into the tub as the water covers my face completely.

No sound—only the roar of the water in my ears. No sight—my eyes are closed tight. Feeling cut off from the world is a wonderful feeling—even if only for a few minutes. Those minutes depend on the length of time I can hold my breath—sometimes a minute, sometimes a bit more. It is enough. Abruptly I am roused from my seclusion by a hand lightly touching my hand. Water splashes all over the bathroom—walls and floors, as I jump up not knowing what to expect to see.

I rub my eyes to clear the water and there he is sitting on the edge of the tub where only moments earlier I had been sitting. He, too, was covered in water.

"I am so sorry," I say as my apology meets his kind eyes and his seductive smile.

"No problem. I didn't mean to startle you. I—I just couldn't help myself, I had to touch your soft skin. I thought your hand would be the least intrusive place to touch."

Bret reaches up and touches my face. Suddenly there is nothing in the world but him as my body involuntarily responds to his touch. I can think of nothing but how badly I want to be with him again. I know that he knows exactly what he is doing—he is doing this intentionally.

"You look so beautiful. You were spectacular last night—the best I have ever had. May I join you?"

"Um—sure, of course." I smile and continue, "It is your apartment, your bathroom. I hope you don't mind. I just really wanted a hot bath." I sit up and make room for this amazing man to sit behind me.

Oh wow—he slides into the black and white porcelain tub behind me. His package brushes up against my ass and I tremble. He slides down further into the tub and presses himself tightly against me as he reaches up and gently coaxes me back against him. My head rests on his muscular chest and I hear the thump, thump, thump of his heart. I feel the rise and fall of his chest. It feels perfect—it is a moment I don't ever want to end. I never want to leave his side.

His deep voice is comforting as he asks, "Did you get my message this morning?" he pointed to the mirror.

"I did. But when and why? How did you know I would see it?"

"I have been with many women and one thing I have learned is that they always go to the bathroom for a hot bath or shower after a night with me."

I know he is smiling, I can hear it in the way he speaks.

"How many women exactly have had the pleasure of bathing with you—being here where I am right now," I say with obvious jealousy in my tone.

"Oh, Mia. Actually there have been many, many women take a bath in this tub before— how many I'm really not sure."

"Hum," I sigh quietly biting back tears.

Bret can tell—I know he can. *Damn it—please don't look at me,* I think.

Bret rises up and coaxes me into a sitting position; he takes my chin between his thumb and index finger and turns my head to face him. That isn't enough—he tips my head back forcing my eyes to meet his.

"Sweet Mia, don't cry," he whispers as he wipes a lone tear from my face that escaped to spite all of my efforts to hold it captive. "There have been many women to bathe in this tub, but I have never bathed with any of them—only you."

I smile. Me being the only one to bathe with him helps a little but knowing that he had been with many still hurts. Wait a minute, that's the pot calling the kettle black, I have been with other men and in both their beds and my own. Why does it bother me so that he has been with other women? And I just met him last night.

I get lost in Bret's eyes as he searches for something in mine—what, I don't know. He leans in and kisses me passionately. I am swept away by his kisses as they become more intense. He swiftly pulls me around to where I am in a sitting position on him and he lies back. I know exactly where this is going and I can't wait.

His hard manhood is pressing against my ass. I rise up slightly and position myself just on the head of his penis. I slide down slowly and to my surprise he gasps. That makes me more excited. The warm water sloshes back and forth covering the floor as it splashes out with every thrust. I ride him for only a few minutes before he totally takes over and grabs me by the hips. He holds me into place as he thrusts himself in and out over and over with his sweet assault on me. My breasts bounce with a pulling sensation and my knees bang against the side of the tub, but that's okay—I can take it.

Finally, with one last thrust he pulls me down hard on his erect penis and penetrates me to the deepest point possible, I scream out. I throw my head back and have that immaculate orgasm. As my pussy contracts on his cock he moans. I then collapse on his chest. The thump, thump, thump of his heartbeat is so much faster now. And the rise and fall of chest is faster and deeper. We lie there for what seems like an eternity.

As my ear presses against his chest Bret's voice is deep and muffled as he speaks. "Come on, let's get washed. I know you must be famished." Then he coaxes me unto my knees facing him.

He reaches up and brushes stray hairs that are covering my eyes back behind my ears. Bret rubs my cheeks and I know he feels something for me. Bret takes a washcloth and lathers it. The excitement grows in me once again as he washes between my legs. He takes his time and I know he is tormenting me intentionally. I moan with pleasure and he smiles. Bret takes his time as he washes every inch of my body. Then he coaxes me back to wash my hair and I breathe in his sweet breath as he leans over me—his face only an inch or so away from mine.

He finishes with me and I take my turn washing him. I take special care with his cock and balls. As I lean over to wash his hair my breasts brush against his chin and turn us both on.

"Naughty girl, you shouldn't do that. If you do, it's going to be longer before you get your breakfast," Bret smiles.

Bret reaches out and plucks one of the monogrammed towels from the towel rack on the wall beside the sink.

"Here, I think we are both thoroughly cleansed."

Bret stands and holds his hand down to me. I take it feeling like a lady taking the hand of a gentleman. I had never really been treated with such affection and courteousness before. It's a strange feeling, isn't this merely a one-night stand. Last night I was sure that's all it was going to be—now I'm not so sure.

My eyes close and I enjoy the bliss as Bret takes the oversized fluffy white towel and dries every inch of my body slowly with conviction.

"Um," an involuntary moan escapes the depths of my throat.

My eyes immediately pop open when I realize what I have done.

"Sorry. It—it just, well it's a relaxing feeling," I say as I smile then bite my lower lip in embarrassment.

"That's okay. I'm happy to have such an affect on you," Bret says as his smile widens.

I know he is very pleased with the affect he's had on me.

Now that he has finished drying me, he dries himself but not nearly with the effort he put into pampering me. In a flash he is finished and steps from the tub. And once again he holds his hand out to me. I take a minute to revel in the wonderful way that I feel right now at this moment just knowing that there will never be another moment like this. I know he can tell what I am thinking.

He smiles, "Mia, there will be many more opportunities for you to use this tub if you like it that much. Come on, let's eat."

My heart skips a beat thinking this must surely be an invitation to come back. I reach out and take his hand and he carefully helps me out of the tub. I am totally shocked by how cool the floor is under my feet. Cold chills run all over my body leaving noticeable goose bumps everywhere.

"Come on let me get you a pair of socks and a bath robe," Bret says as he holds the towel out and encircles me with it; he pulls me close into his body wrapping his arm around me. His body pressed against mine he leads me back toward the bedroom; I notice things I hadn't noticed earlier. There were no pictures of people—no parents, no siblings, no friends, no Bret. That's odd; I have pictures of practically everyone I know all about my apartment. Maybe he is orphaned; maybe he has no one.

This apartment is so impersonal. My apartment is a scattered mess. Maybe he is just a clean freak. As the bedroom door comes into view I see something in a room we are passing; it is a messy room filled with beautifully painted canvases, paint, paint brushes, cleaning cloths, etc. I stop dead in my tracks. The door to this room was closed when I had gone in search of the bathroom so I had not noticed the beautiful paintings before.

"You're an artist?" I ask with a surprised tone in my voice.

"Yes. You act surprised." His smile is breathtaking.

"Well, I just didn't picture you for the artist type that's all. Can I see some of your work?"

"Be my guest," he says as he bows slightly and extends his arm toward the room.

Walking past him and into the room slowly I make my way to first painting and then the next. I am so amazed and I am so drawn in to his work that I forget to say anything. The pictures are of beautiful women—must be his muses, women he has slept with I'm sure. I wonder if I will be added to his collection later. The spectacular landscapes are of places that I recognize and others I do not.

He waits patiently as I examine every painting and every sketch. Feeling his eyes upon me I return the last sketch to the drawing table and turn to see Bret smiling with his arms crossed in front of his chest and obvious pride splayed across his face. Oh this man is charming.

"These are magnificent. You are extremely talented," the words just kind of spill from my mouth awkwardly.

"Thank you. This is actually my job. I paint on commission and I sell my work at art galleries as well."

He extends his had to me and I take it. It is warm and gentle. His touch is electrifying. Hand in hand we walk out of the room and toward the kitchen, stopping momentarily to retrieve an oversized fuzzy robe and a pair or women's bobby socks for me, and a pair of jeans for him. The kitchen is also impersonal. No special coffee mugs or crazy kitchen art like roosters or cows. The appliances are all stainless steel and are pressed against more stark white walls, counter tops and cabinets. The table matches the kitchen perfectly being stainless steel and glass. Everything is so contemporary and modern—so different from my taste.

"Here have seat," Bret says as he pulls a stainless steel framed and white canvassed covered chair from the table.

I smile at him and sit as he pushes me up to the table.

"So you can cook too, huh?" I ask.

"Oh, I have many talents. So what would you like?" he asks as he opens the refrigerator.

"Um—fruit and toast with some juice would be just fine. I don't want to put you out."

"Oh Mia," he says as he sticks his head in the refrigerator pulling out several items. "You need a bit more that fruit and toast. You are going to run this morning aren't you?"

My eyes widen. *Okay how does he know I run every morning?*

"Well—I had planned on it. How did you know?" I ask with bewilderment in my voice.

"I just assumed. You have a runner's body. And you kept up well with me last night," he smiles at me peeping over the refrigerator door.

He places tofu, soy milk and a few other groceries on the counter. "I will prepare scrambled tofu with spinach and mushrooms, toast, a piece of sausage alternative, and your fruit. Does that sound okay?" he asks as he begins slicing mushrooms.

"Sure," is all I can manage.

He pulls out the skillets, the spatulas, turns on the stove and begins to cook like a master chef. I watch his stunning and graceful body move about pulling plates from the cupboard and silverware from a nearby drawer to set two places—one for me and one for him. *Walla! —breakfast is served.*

He pours my juice and his soy milk and serves our breakfast. I'm not aware of just how hungry I am until I see and smell this delectable breakfast set in front of me. My mouth waters almost as much for this scrumptious plate of food as it did for his divine body earlier this morning.

"Now eat up. We can run through the park together and afterward we can come back here and shower. I can drop you off at work on my way to the gallery."

Mind my flounders trying to decide whether to be flattered or terrified that Bret knows so much about me and I still only know his first name and what he has shared with me at the club last night and here at his apartment.

"How do you know so much about me? How do you know that I am vegan, that I run through the park every morning and where I work? And what am I supposed to wear to run in? I need a change of clothes unless you have been shopping for me as well."

"I actually have been shopping for you. I bought the groceries that you like and I bought spare clothes for you. I know your name is Mia Vanderbilt and I know that you work as a photographer at Still Lense Photography. I know that you don't eat meat, you frequent clubs and your best friend is Amy Watson.

It all made sense now—*Amy.*

"Amy set this all up?"

"Well not really. I had come by the photography studio one day a few months ago. You were working hard and didn't even know anyone else was in the world that day. I fell in love with you. I had known Amy for about a year and I asked her for the down low on you."

"So hooking up last night was no accident?"

"Well—I wouldn't say that. Meeting you was no accident but hitting it off so well was very unexpected. Amy told me you like to take it slow with guys and hadn't been in a relationship for a couple of years. So you coming back here and spending the night with me was a total surprise."

I can't decide whether I should be annoyed or honored that this man went to so much trouble to please me and to be with me.

"Okay. I don't know what to do with all of this information," I say as I push my chair away from the table. "Thank you for last night, for the bath and breakfast but I think I'm going to leave now. I need some time to ponder this situation."

"Mia, please don't go. I'm sorry. I shouldn't have come on so strong and stalker type. I just wanted to please you. Mia," he calls out as he grabs hold of my arm causing the robe to slide down off of my shoulder.

I stop briefly and just look at him then slowly pull the robe back over my naked flesh. And I see something in his eyes that surprises me—fear and desperation. He gently releases my arm and I turn and walk into the bedroom. I quickly dress. I am slightly disappointed that he doesn't try harder to get me to stay and forgive him. I grab my purse and briskly make my way to the front door. I am surprised to see him sitting at the kitchen table with his head in hand. He never looks up as I open the door and walk out. As I close the door behind me I can't help but feel slight regret for what I have just done. I lean my face against the door and place my hands on it half expecting him to open in and me fall into his arms. I don't want to leave but I have to stand my ground. He has to know that this is manipulation, and I won't be manipulated. I imagine Bret standing on the other side of the door—head and hands resting upon it. Bret—Bret what? I still don't know his last name. In fact, I'm unsure of where I am exactly. And Amy—wait until I get to work.

I brood and bitch all the way back to my apartment, which is only three blocks uptown. Damn he lives way too close. I grab clean clothes, slap on a bit of makeup to brighten up my violet eyes and bush out my hair. I keep thinking I should get a short trendy do with blue streaks that would be quite visible shining through my coal black locks. I think it would fit me just fine but Amy chastises me every time I mention it.

Since I didn't get my morning jog in I pull my bicycle from the closet. With my purse and camera in my backpack I sling it across my shoulders and roll my bicycle into the hallway. I secure my door and drop the key in my sport bra just between my boobs. I know it will be sweaty when I get to the studio but that's okay—I know I won't lose it there.

I continue brooding all the way to the studio, which is eight blocks in the opposite direction—down town. I am so pissed that I get there in almost half the time it should take. I lock my bicycle down in the front. Fishing the key from my sticky boobs, I walk through the door and who is the first to greet me—Amy.

"Hey Mia, so how'd it go last night?" she asks in a sweet chipper voice flowing from behind her innocent smile.

"Oh, Amy we have a lot to talk about," I snipe and grab her by the arm. In an instant she knows the jig is up.

"Um—what did Bret tell you?" she trips over her words.

"Pretty much everything."

"Please don't be mad. He is a great guy. I can't believe he told you. I told him you would have a bad reaction to this," she says as she is wringing her hands.

"He didn't have much of a choice after he basically told me he had been stalking me. I can't believe you would do this to me," I squawk at her.

I feel like someone kicked me in the stomach when her eyes begin to tear up. Hurting her is the last thing I want to do; I am just so angry and hurt myself.

Her words are barely audible when she bows her head and simply says, "I'm sorry Mia. I didn't mean to hurt you."

What the Hell is wrong with me? Why am I so pissed? My best friend set me up with the perfect guy and we hit it off. I should be thanking her and fucking him. I am so stupid.

Guilt ridden I gently take her by the hand and pull her closely and hug her. She wraps her arms around me until I can barely breathe.

"Oh, so you forgive me?"

"Yes. But why would you go behind my back?"

"I didn't want to. Bret is very persuasive. He fell head over heels for you. He just wanted to make certain that when you guys met it would be phenomenal—something you would never forget. I guess he went a little too far."

"I got to think about this. I'm going on to do some work on the computer I have some pics to tweak and then I have a shoot later today. We will talk more later."

"One thing…did you break his heart this morning?"

"I—I don't know," I respond with regret filling me. "Why? Does it matter?"

"Well—yeah. He is a great guy."

I turn and walk away before I burst into tears. My day is filled with this guilt from the way I treated this wonderful man and the way I treated my best friend weighing heavy on my mind. My day is pretty unproductive.

A couple of days pass avoiding Amy from shame and guilt, not from anger. I can't sleep at night, can't eat and I have gotten absolutely no work done. I am a total mess. When I go into to work on the third morning after that wonderful night with Bret I decide I have to make things right with Amy. I find her and pull her aside as soon as I go into work.

"Amy. I am so sorry. I feel just terrible."

I automatically pull her close for a hug as tears rolls down both our faces.

"Oh my God, I am so happy. I thought for sure that you hated me. I was so upset knowing that you were mad at me," Amy says between tear-filled gasps.

"Amy. I was only mad at you for about five seconds. I was ashamed for the way I acted. I just felt so guilty I couldn't face you. I am so sorry. Will you ever forgive me?"

I am crying so hard at this point that poor Amy can barely understand what I am saying through all of the heaves and gasps.

"Of course I forgive you. You are my best friend— the sister I never had. I love you. I only told Bret about you because he is such a wonderful guy. I have been told he used to be a real womanizer but not in the past year—not since around the time he came in here for the first time. And Andy told me that he has never had a long-term relationship.

Andy would know because they have been friends for about five years."

"Do you really trust Andy?"

"Of course I do. We have been going out for a year and a half and I know he is the one. I trust him with my life. He wouldn't lie about something like this—not to me."

I just stand silently knowing what a huge mistake I have made.

Amy finally says something to break the long silence. "So what are you going to do—about Bret?"

"I'm not sure. I don't know how I could ever face him after my childish behavior. I was a total bitch. He will never want to see me again—no matter how crazy he was about me. He can't possibly be crazy about me now. And besides I haven't heard from him since I stormed out that morning."

Regret fills my eyes and trickles across my tongue as my voice quivers.

"You might be surprised. Do you want me to ask Andy if he has talked to him—see if I can get any info?"

"Thanks, but no. If he does hate me I would rather not know it straight up."

I force a smile through a tear stricken face. And turn to walk away.

Amy grabs my arm and just gives me this apathetic look. I know exactly what she is thinking but I am finished crying for the day—Hell, for the year. I never let myself get this vulnerable. I hate for people to portray me as weak. I have worked so hard to be independent and strong—like an Amazon. I am an Amazon. I smile slightly at that internal thought. And walk away as her grasps loosens to release me from her pity.

I feel much better about Amy and myself but Bret is still weighing heavy on my mind.

A few weeks pass and I muddle through pretty much every day forcing myself to do what needs to be done. I'm not even running every morning—this used to be my mediation time. Now all I can think about is Bret and how badly I messed things up.

It has been a couple of weeks and walking to work I feel this surge of energy as I see Bret walking into Still Lense Photography. *Oh my God, he has come to forgive me and to ask me for another chance.* I am several people behind him so he doesn't see me. I finally make my way through the door and look all around making my way to my small office. Then I spot him and my heart sinks.

I throw my stuff just inside my office door and run to the bathroom, eyes fill with tears that I just can't keep captive. The sight of him holding that young beautiful woman around the waist as they look at my photos on the wall is more than I can bear. I know it—he is going to either set up a shoot for me to photograph her or he is buying her a piece of my work. *Of all the nerve.*

They look so happy. He didn't care anything for me. He moved on fast enough.

After a few minutes of drying tears, I look up to see that bitch standing in front of me—that bitch who was just in Bret's arms. *AHH,* I just want to yell. But I don't. I am a strong woman—an Amazon who does not need a man. *Screw him!*

Damn it, the bitch is looking at me sympathetically. I know she is going to say something and I am just not in the mood for it.

"Hey, I know it's none of my business but are you alright? I'm Janie Barker."

The bitch extends her hand. She seems so nice. It's not her fault Bret is a jerk. I immediately feel at ease—she has such kind eyes and caring voice.

"I'm fine. Thank you. I'm Mia Vanderbilt."

.

"Pardon me for saying so but you really don't look fine. Is it a guy?" She pauses for a minute like she is hit with an empathy. "Wait, did you say Mia?"

"Yes," I stammer.

"I was actually looking at some of work out front. My cousin told me about you and thought I might like it. He offered to buy one of your pieces so he brought me in this morning to pick a photo—"

I interrupt her before she can finish. Enthusiastically I quickly ask, "So Bret is your cousin?"

"Yes." It takes her a minute but when she sees my immediate mood change at this newfound knowledge she pieces things together. "Wait a minute, you thought Bret and I were together? Is this why you are so upset? Oh, I get it. He told me about a girl he met a few weeks ago. Is that you?"

"I guess. I met him a few weeks ago. But we haven't seen each other since," I admit.

"Well you should know that you broke his heart. If you like him this much, you should really tell him," Janie says sternly.

I am surprised in Janie's sudden change in tone and attitude.

"I guess I should rejoin Bret and pick my photo."

Janie turns to walk away and for some odd reason I did something so out of character, I grab Janie by the arm. Janie stops in her tracks, turns and looks at me puzzled.

"I didn't mean to break his heart—really."

"Well, that's between you and Bret. It is really none of my business."

"Please let me explain."

"There is really no need," Janie says as she tries to pull her arm away.

I refuse to let go. "I really do need to explain."

"Okay then, but it really is none of my business. If it will make you feel better, start talking."

I loosen my hold on Janie and tell her what had happened the night I met Bret, minus the intimate details. I explain how I felt like I had been betrayed, tricked and stalked but in spite of all of that I really like him.

"You should really be telling Bret how you feel, not me. I know I am a bit biased because he is my cousin and we are very close but he is a great guy," Janie says as her tone once again softens as she reaches out her hand to me.

I slowly reach up and take Janie's hand. Janie puts her arm around my waist. I hate that I feel vulnerable once again. I hate that I am letting a total stranger comfort me, but there is just something about Janie that makes my guard lower.

"I really don't know what to say to him. I feel terrible."

"Just tell him what you told me—about how you feel about him and about the way things went down that morning."

They walk toward Bret. He can't believe what he is seeing—strong Mia in tears and so fragile in the arms of his cousin.

"Mia, are you alright? What's wrong?"

Janie passes me off to Bret and walks away to examine more of the photos that line the walls of the studio giving us a chance to reconcile.

I fall into Bret's arms and hold tightly—as if I will fall if I don't cling to him.

"Is there somewhere we can talk?" Bret asks.

"My office."

I gesture toward my office with my hand, we go in but do not sit. I stay close in his arms. I begin to tell him everything that I feel, everything thing that I have felt for the past two and a half weeks. How I regret being so stupid and stubborn. He doesn't really say anything. He just smiles at me, tilts my head back slightly and kisses me deeply. My knees go week and I fall into him. Nothing else matters—only Bret. I totally forget where we are as everyone in the studio watches.

Amy walks over and clears her throat. "Uh-um. Mia why don't you take the day off?"

I smile at Amy and then at Bret. "I think I will."

Amy smiles and closes the door behind her.

"Do you have time for me today?" I ask.

"I have all the time in the world for you Mia. What do you want to do?" Bret takes my hand, brings it to his lips and kisses it.

"Well, my apartment is closer. Can we go back there?"

"We can do whatever you want?"

I grab my things and take Bret's hand. Bret buys Janie the photo she picks out. It is actually my favorite, a photo of a lonely tree in the midst of nowhere. It is in negative colors and is a very solemn photo. He gives the studio Janie's address so they can have the photo couriered over. We tell Janie goodbye and she goes on to more shopping up the street. We tell Amy goodbye and she goes back to work. Bret and I walking hand in hand back to my apartment I can barely contain myself because I know what is inevitable once we reach my place.

We catch up on what has happened to each of us in the past two and a half weeks. We are standing in front of my apartment door before we know it as I fumble nervously with my keys. Bret just watches with a smile until I finally get the damn door open.

I walk in first and lay my keys and purse on the chair next to the front door as Bret closes and locks it behind us. He takes me in his arms and his hands wander over my entire body as he kisses me first with only open mouth and then sliding his tongue past my lips exploring every inch of my mouth. I can barely breath and I am already wet with excitement. I quickly lead him to my bedroom.

He reaches down and rubs between my legs the friction causing me to become wetter. My face flushes and I can feel my nipples becoming hard against my bra—they ache. I hear the distinct sound of a zipper and soon realize it is the sound of my zipper. Bret slides his hand in the front of my pants and his fingers under my panties until they are pressing firmly against my clit. He moves his fingers around slowly causing me to involuntarily moan.

I reach down and pull his hand further back until it is at my opening. Then I push his hand in an upward motion causing a finger to slide into me slightly.

Bret's kisses deepen as he forces his finger deeper. I gasp. He stops. I beg for him not to stop—I beg for more.

He whispers in my ear, "More fingers?"

I gasp, "Yes, please."

He slides another finger inside me and moves them in and out as much as he can due to the restriction of my pants. After a few minutes he abruptly pulls his fingers out of me and his hand out of my pants. A sudden fear comes over me the fear he is going to stop.

Brent leans down and gently release one foot and then the other from my shoes then without warning he pulls my pants and panties off in one fell swoop. He unbuttons my top and throws it to the ground and unclasps my bra and tosses it to the side. I am totally naked—totally exposed. He discards all of his clothes in seconds flat.

My back is cooled from the wall that I am pinned against by Bret's body. He kisses me again but this time he leaves a trail of searing kisses from my mouth down my neck stopping for a few minutes giving both breast equal attention; then moves downward across my stomach and his lips find a resting spot at my clit. His hot tongue caresses me slowly. He spreads my legs so that he can get closer. Bret slides his tongue into my opening and forces it in and out of me over and over. I know I will die from the pleasure.

Just when I think I can't take anymore he moves his tongue back to my clit and runs his hand up my leg forcing two of his fingers into me. I pull his head closer to me and I grind down on his hand forcing his fingers deeper. Then without warning he forces another finger in me causing a painful but pleasurable stretching sensation. I moan and call out for more. Bret obliges by sliding in a fourth finger and I grind down hard forcing his fingers into me up to his hand. I scream out in pleasure as he thrusts his fingers in and out over and over. I am so wet that my cum is dripping down his hand. He chews my clit lightly between his teeth.

"Oh baby do you like that? I have more for you. Just be patient," he moans through gritted teeth.

Without warning he removes his fingers and forces me to my knees. His cock is huge and in my face. He tips my head back and thrust his dick inside my mouth.

"Try some of me now," he moans.

Bret fucks my mouth over and over until I can't breathe. I am gasping for breath and gagging from his engorged penis. Just before he cums he pulls out and lays me down on the bed.

Bret quickly positions himself over me and slides his cock deep within me and pounds the hell out me. He thrusts in and out over and over. I know I have cum at least four times. Finally, he releases in me. I can feel the warmth explode within me. He collapses on top of me. We are both hot, sweaty and totally out of breath.

He raises up his head smiles at me and asks in a deep sultry voice, "Did I rock your world?"

"Oh yes. A couple of times actually." I smile and close my eyes.

I listlessly fall asleep in his arms to be awakened a few hours later to the smell of a wonderful lunch. I roll over to put my arm across Bret's chest but he is not there. I begin to become lucid and realize that wonderful smell must be Bret's cooking. I take a deep breath roll over onto my back and smile reveling in the moment of having spent the past several hours in this man's arms and having him prepare me a meal I know it'll be fit for royalty—it has to be the way it smells.

I slowly pull myself up into a sitting position and push the sheets back exposing my naked and sticky body. I ease my legs over the side of the bed letting my feet touch the cool hardwood floor. It is a refreshing feeling—the coolness rushes from my toes throughout my entire body giving me tiny chill bumps all over. This rush of coolness brings my nipples to a salute. I rub them with a vain attempt at reducing their size—it does not work.

I finally make my way to the bathroom, which is attached to my bedroom. As I prepare for my shower I remember Bret's bathroom and how different there are in contrast. Mine has hardwood floors, it has a pedestal tub with a shower, and the sink is an old sink that sets up on posts and has a curtain around the base. The window is adorned with cozy floral curtains that are pulled back to let as much sunlight in as possible. I keep small potted plants in the window to bring a little life to that room.

As I am adjusting my shower water, I notice a wet towel hanging very neatly across the towel rack—Bret had already showered. I smile and go on with my shower. The warm water causing more chill bumps that keep my nipples erect. When I finish my shower I opt to use the towel Bret had used instead of a clean dry towel. I just wanted that intimacy of sharing something so personal—kind of like eating or drinking after someone or using their toothbrush.

I fumble clumsily through clothes that are unfolded in my dresser drawers until I find a pair of jeans and a button up cotton top. I elect to omit bra and panties but slip on a pair of house shoes—I can't stand for my feet to be cold.

I look in the mirror to check my appearance. I decide it's not that great—my mascara is smeared under my eyes and my hair is a total mess. I hurry back to the bathroom and clean my eyes with makeup remover and run a brush through my hair only to fluff it back out with my hands giving a slightly messy look. I brush my teeth, grab deodorant and spritz some Channel No. 5 on my neck and wrists. *Okay,* I think to myself, *this is much better.*

I quietly walk into the kitchen behind Bret. I slide my arms around his waist and lay my face against his back. He doesn't flinch.

"Well, I wasn't sure whether I should make you lunch or dinner. I'm happy you made it for lunch," he says in that sultry voice.

He puts down the spatula he is cooking with and turns to gather me in his arms. He envelopes me and I just melt into him.

"This feels so good," I say as I keep my head close to his chest.

"It definitely does, much better than last time when you stormed out and I thought I had lost you before I ever had the chance to really have you. I know it was wrong to sneak around behind your back to find out about you, but I just wanted to make certain that I did everything right. I didn't want to take a chance on screwing up my chance with you," he says as he kisses the top of my head.

I smile as I listen to the rhythmic beating of this wonderful man's heart. "I can't apologize enough for blowing up. Thank you for giving me another chance."

This wonderful moment is interrupted by the loud ring of Bret's cell phone. He pulls away and sighs.

"I should probably get that."

"Sure," I say not really wanting to leave his arms, not even for a moment.

Bret walks into the living room and retrieves his phone from the coffee table. He looks at the phone pensively almost reluctantly.

"It's business, I should take it out there," he says as he gestures toward the front door.

I just nod my head and smile. It is a forced smile. I feel that he is hiding something from me but then again it is business, his business and none of mine. Still it eats away at me.

Bret opens the front door and steps outside the relentless ringing of the phone screaming to be answered. He pulls the door shut behind him. I grab an empty juice glass from the table and am at the front door in seconds. I have to know what is so private, what he is hiding. I put the glass to the door and my ear to the glass so that the conversation outside is better amplified.

"What do you want? I told you I was busy today and not to call me. This is really not a good time. Yes. Yes of course. I do care about you but I told you I can't see you today. Well, it's complicated. I thought you understood."

There is a long pause then Bret says to the person on the other end, "I have to go now. I will talk to you tonight."

My heart sinks. He is seeing someone else. He is still a player. What kind of game is he playing? I am pissed but don't show it this time. I jumped to conclusions the first time we were together and let him know it. I am not going to make that mistake again. I have to find out who was on the other side of that conversation.

As I hear the conversation end I run back to the kitchen and stand by the sink still holding the glass as Bret walks in. He looks upset, strained and unhinged. I sit the glass down and walk over to him. Maybe I was all wrong about this conversation, it was one sided after all.

"What is it? Is everything alright?" I ask as I touch his arm.

He shakes his head slightly. "Um, no. I mean yes. It's complicated. I really don't want to get into it. I just want to enjoy my time with you. Okay?"

"Sure."

Bret smiles and pulls me in close for a hug. It is different than the way he held me before. This time it feels as though he is searching for something in me to relieve his angst. I let him hold me as long as he needs to. To be honest I never want him to let go.

He pulls back only enough to see my face. "Okay, I am starving. How about you?"

"I am a bit hungry," I smile.

Bret finishes cooking and serves us. We eat and the mood lightens as conversation continues. We laugh and talk and I almost completely forget the phone call—until Bret's phone rings again. He picks it up and looks at it. He once again has that strange look about his face.

"Do you need to take that? I can leave if you want privacy." I start to stand.

He takes me hand, "No. Please. I don't need to take this."

He hits the fuck you button on the phone. It almost immediately rings again. This time he turns the phone off.

"I don't mean to be nosey but…"

"It's just someone who needs a friend but they are way too needy and to be honest I think the best thing for them is a good therapist," Bret smiles but it is a sad kind of smile.

I still feel a pang of jealousy and suspicion. I can't help it—I do not have a good track record with men. I try not to let Bret see how upsetting these mysterious phone calls are to me.

"What do you say we got to the park for a while?" Bret suggests.

I ponder this idea for a long moment.

"Mia? What do you say?"

I smile and agree. "Sure. Sounds like fun."

"Then we can swing by my place for me to change clothes and then back here for you to change," Bret suggests.

"Then what?" I ask.

"Then I take you out to dinner." Bret smiles and winks at me.

"That sounds great." I am feeling much better now as Bret's undivided attention is focused on me.

We finish getting ready and head out to the park. It is a sunny day, flowers are in full bloom and I am all smiles as Bret and I walk hand in hand. We find a park bench under a beautiful shade tree.

"Shall we stop here?" Bret asks as he gestures toward a wooden and wrought iron bench.

I smile and nod as I take a seat. Bret places his arm around me as he sits beside me. I snuggle close to him and it feels good. We talk and learn much about each other. It is wonderful having him open up and tell me about his life. We talk, laugh and watch people and their pets as they stroll by.

A shrill voice cut through me peace and pleasure as a voluptuous and, obviously wealthy, woman strolls over arms open.

"Cinnamon?" Bret stammers out in surprise.

"Oh, my sweetums I have tried to get you on the phone all day. Something must be wrong with it. I would call the phone company if I were you," Cinnamon says as she leans over and throws her massive half exposed breasts in Bret's face as she wraps her arms around him.

"I am certain that I informed you earlier that I would be unavailable today," Bret sternly declared as he stood.

Cinnamon just won't let go of Bret. Even though he squirms nervously under her grasp, he makes no real effort to break free. I can feel my face turning red and I begin to hear a faint ringing in my ears as I realize this must have been the woman he had spoken too earlier—just before he had turned his phone off.

Cinnamon kisses Bret square on the mouth. This is the last straw—I run as fast as I can from the park. I barely hear the faint sound of Bret's voice calling my name because of the pounding in my ears of my pulse. My chest is tight and everything is a blur as my eyes fill with tears. My face is on fire and my head is pounding. *I have to get home! Run faster! Don't stop no matter how it hurts!* Then I can hear that bitch.

"Bret! Bret, where are going?"

I look over my shoulder to see Bret running.

Oh, God he is going to catch up with me. I can't let him. I have to outrun him. I have to get away.

Luckily I am a bit better runner than he, I have a head start, and traffic slows him to a stop. I am back to my apartment and inside before he catches up to me. Sliding down the door I sit in the floor back against the door and head in hands. The tears flow. I am so stupid. Why did I give him another chance? He is just like all the rest. Men cannot be trusted—

but you can definitely count on them to break your heart.

Pound, pound, pound. "Let me in! Mia, please let me explain!"

"There is no need to explain. Actions speak louder than words. I am not blind—just stupid. I won't let you make a fool out of me for a third time. Just go!" My words are muffled as I scream through my hands still covering my tear stricken face.

"Mia, I'm not trying to make a fool of you. Please let me in. I will sit out here all night if I have to."

Not saying another word, I stand and walk to the bathroom sobbing in my hands, Bret still talking through the door—his words getting less audible with each step I take.

Slowly I slip from my clothing and get into the bathtub, turning on first the hot and then the cold water—adjusting it just right. I lay back and submerge myself in the water until only my nose is out of the water. I use my toes to turn off the water. I lay there in a muffled silence—contemplating it all. How easy it would be to just slid under and let go. Giving in to it all, I do just that—slid completely under and let go. I hold my breath briefly; then exhale that last bit of air emptying my lungs completely. How long can I hold out?

I think about everything in my life as it all fades to black and then nothing.

Wait there is a sound—a muffled crashing sound. Soft warm hands grasp my body and pull me from the water. It's so cold. Loving arms envelop me and I instantly regret my recent decisions—how stupid and impulsive. Thank the goddess Bret didn't just give up on me and go home. He does love me.

My body is like ice as Bret thrusts it upon the floor and begins pounding my chest and breathing into my mouth. Slowly the black fades back into the living and muffled sounds become so clear. The sounds of Bret's frantic begging me not leave him. A cough from a tight and burning chest as water erupts from my mouth and all over Bret's face. He laughs in relief and then scolds from fear.

"What the Hell are you trying to prove?"

I cough more as I try to catch my breath. I sit up slowly and just look at him—the pain in his eyes tears through my heart. I was wrong about him—I just need to follow my heart and leave my logic behind to wallow in self-doubt.

"If you're going to treat me like a child you can just leave now," I struggle to get the words out broken and in gasps.

Bret pulls me close to him and hugs me so tightly I can't breathe.

"Lighten up a bit. I am still trying to catch my breath."

He loosens his grip slightly. "I'm sorry. You scared me so. I love you—I don't want to ever lose you. Will you please tell me what you were thinking?"

My eyes filled with apology meet Bret's.

"That woman, Cinnamon. You have a relationship with her, don't you?"

"No! I mean not now. I had been seeing her until the day I saw you in the studio. I broke it off with her a few days after that. She just won't give up. I have been avoiding her but she stalks me."

"You have been avoiding her, but have you flat out told her you are no longer interested—that there is someone else in your life?" I scold.

"Of course. What kind of ass do you take me for?" Bret defends himself.

"Then maybe it's time for me to have a talk with her myself!" I demand.

I will make that bitch retreat and in a big fucking hurry. She will wish she had never been born if she continues to stalk my lover.

"I have no objections to that at all. I only have one request."

"What's that?" I question through shivering lips.

"Wait a few days until you are over this rage and have a clear head about you." Bret not only begs with his voice but his eyes look so desperate for me to answer yes.

I am speechless for almost a full minute and then finally concede to his request.

"Very well. Do you want to accompany me?"

Bret immediately responds, "I would, only because Cinnamon can be unpredictable and volatile. I don't ever want you to be alone with her. Okay?"

"Okay." I promise not knowing exactly what he meant and at this point not really caring. I am so cold that my body is trembling uncontrollably.

Bret notices how badly I am shivering, "Come on, let's get you dry and warm before you catch your death."

I only nod as he helps me to my feet and vigorously dries me. He towel dries my hair. Finally, he wraps me in an oversized downy towel, holds me closely and walks me to my bedroom where he rummages through my drawers until he finds a fuzzy pair of pajamas.

Holding up a pair of pajamas, he smiles and asks, "Will these work? They look very warm."

I smile back beginning to feel much better about everything, "Yes. Those will be just fine, thank you."

Bret looks deeply into my eyes for a long moment and then drops his gaze to my breasts as he lowers my towel. His look reminds me of a hungry animal. I know what he is wanting but he doesn't make a move. Other than the heavy seductive gaze he is a gentleman. After several minutes he breaks his gaze and helps me into my pajama top and then holds my bottoms as I step into them then pulls them up slowly letting his hands glide from my waist to my breasts brushing up against me as he buttons my top. I have never before been so turned on by being dressed. I want desperately for him to undo what he had just done—rip my clothes off and throw me onto the bed taking whatever he wants from me. Alas he smiles and cups my face in his hands.

"Come on, let's get you warmed up," he turns down my heavy comforter and helps me into bed.

I don't put up a fuss and he slides in beside me pulling the covers up and snuggling in close. I can immediately feel the heat from his body radiating through my clothes. It takes no time for me to warm up.

My angst from earlier gives way to his comforting arms and the events culminating from my momentary lapse of judgment fade into desire. That sweet spot between my legs begins to throb and all I can think about is Bret and how much I ache to feel his cock between my legs. I snuggle in closer and press up against him. He is hard and I know he wants me. It won't take much. I move slightly rubbing my breasts against his chest. I am face to face with him breathing in his sweet intoxicating exhalation.

Bret makes his move and closes in fast. I feel his mouth come down hard upon mine leaving me weak and breathless. Excitement grows within me the deeper his tongue ventures into my mouth. Soon he leaves a searing trail of kisses down my neck and across each breast—giving each one equal attention before moving down across my stomach and to my vagina. My back arches involuntarily and I feel his breath on my thigh as he lets out a tiny snicker. He takes no time in resuming his attention to where it belongs. His tongue sweeps across my opening like wet velvet—making me cum instantly. I know I am filling his mouth—I have to be.

Finally, when I feel I can take no more Bret moves back up leaving a searing trail with his tongue until he once again finds my mouth. His kisses are deep and passionate. He positions himself exactly where I want him to be. And in one quick flash he thrusts himself into me. I fall into the abyss of ecstasy. I completely loose myself to Bret. One last thrust and a sexy moan emerges from Bret.

We fall asleep in one another's arms. And I forget all the craziness from the past few hours. All I feel is comfort and relief. Bret is slumbering soundly as I awake to a knocking on the door.

I slide out from under his arm and slip from the covers careful not to disturb Bret. I pull on the fuzzy pajamas and close the bedroom door. Make my way slowly to the door wondering who it could possibly be. I notice the room is dark except for a tiny sliver of light from a street lamp is dancing in from between where the drapes are pushed together. I can see the hands on the wall clock hanging above the couch. It says 3:45. I can't believe that we had slept so long. It was already 3:45 AM. Now I really wonder who the Hell it could be.

I creep over to the door and look out the peephole but see no one. Maybe I had been dreaming. I turn to walk back to the bedroom but a slightly louder knock than before startles me. I turn and quickly look out once again. But again no one. Now my curiosity gets the better of me and knowing better I open the door anyway. To my surprise I am rushed and pushed back into the apartment.

I panic not knowing what to do. I hear the door being locked so I take this opportunity to find the lights. As the lights illuminate the room I see a familiar face—the face of Cinnamon.

"What the Hell are you doing here?" I demand.

"Oh don't play Miss Innocent. I know you seduced Bret from me. But I am here to put an end to this," she declared.

My panic stricken heart races as I see the simmering of a long blade as it emerges from under her jacket. I am so wishing that I had left the bedroom door open. I know my best bet is to get back to the bedroom where Bret is. It's obvious she doesn't know he's here. The only problem is she is standing between me and my escape route. I fake left and then try to jut around her on the right but she's too quick for me.

I feel an immediate sharp pain in my left side as a warmth flows down my lower side and legs. I crumble to the ground hoping that she will just go and Bret will wake. I can see in Cinnamon's eyes that she has big plans for me tonight. Fear floods my body as I see her blade raise above her head. It's ironic that only a few hours earlier I was the one choosing to end my life but now I desperately want to live.

I know my end is near as I see the blade plummeting toward my chest. I close my eyes and wait. Suddenly I hear a moan and a body upon mine. I heard the most precious voice ever.

"Mia, are you okay?" Bret asks as he rolled Cinnamon off of me.

Before I can say a word I hear Bret.

"Oh my God! Here press this down as tight as you can," he said as he pulls his shirt off and balls it up tightly and presses it hard against my side. "I'm going to call an ambulance and the police."

I grab is hand and pull him back to me. "What about Cinnamon?"

"Don't worry about her. She will never hurt you again," Bret says and then kisses my forehead before he goes to the phone.

I look over and see that Cinnamon is not breathing and see the back of her head is soaked in blood. There is a lamp lying on the floor beside her.

Bret does really love me—he killed for me.

Other work by
Jossette Devereaux

The Pagan And The Prince

www.ingramcontent.com/pod-product-compliance
Lightning Source LLC
Chambersburg PA
CBHW020320150626
46552CB00022B/3038